# It never hurts to ask...

"And how's the greatest-dad-in-the-history-of-dads feeling today?" D.J. wanted to know.

Danny cocked his head. "Suspicious," he said.

D.J. pulled a chair out from the kitchen table. "Have a seat, Dad. Make yourself comfortable."

"Careful, Dad," Stephanie warned. "She wants money—and lots of it."

D.J. stared at her sister. "How did you know?" she asked.

"Deej, we go back eight years," said Stephanie. "Face it—we all know when it's kiss-up time."

Stephanie finished her snack and left D.J. to her begging.

"All right . . ."—Danny took out his wallet—"how much?"

# FULL HOUSE

## Way to Go, Chipmunk Cheeks

by Bonnie Worth
Based on the series *FULL HOUSE*™ *created by*
Jeff Franklin
*and on episodes written by:*
Jeff Franklin
Martie Cook
Marc Warren & Dennis Rinsler

**A PARACHUTE PRESS BOOK**

Parachute Press, Inc.
156 Fifth Avenue
New York, NY 10010

ISBN: 0-938753-57-6
Printed in the United States of America
September 1991
10  9  8  7  6  5  4  3  2  1

# ONE

**D.J. Tanner** lay sprawled out on her bed, surrounded by half a dozen open magazines. Within arm's reach sat a pair of scissors, a pot of glue, a piece of cardboard, and—best of all—a brand-new bag of cookies. Chocolate chip—D.J.'s cookie of the week.

D.J. reached into the bag for a cookie before cutting out a photo of a chimpanzee wearing a bonnet. This humor magazine was excellent. She also had magazines on fashion, sports, cars, rock stars, and movies. Brushing crumbs from the chimp's face, she glued the picture to the cardboard and laughed to herself. "Why, Kimmy," she said. "I never *knew* you could look so dashing in a hat!"

D.J. was making a collage for her best friend Kimmy's fourteenth birthday, which was in two weeks. Stephanie, D.J.'s "overly mature" kid sister, marched into the bedroom that the two of them shared.

"You look like you could use a little musical accompaniment," Stephanie announced. She blew into her new reed flute. A few notes that sounded like "On Top of Old Smokey," came out.

D.J. winced. "Do you have to play that in here, Stef?" she asked.

Looking offended, Stephanie lowered the instrument. "This happens to be my homework for music appreciation."

"Yeah?" said D.J. "Well, when it happens to be music, I'll appreciate it. Now can't you go practice somewhere else? Preferably in a soundproof room? I'm making Kimmy's card."

Just then, Kimmy Gibbler herself waltzed in. As usual, her sense of timing was perfect. "Hi, guys," she said, grinning.

"Kimmy!" D.J. scrambled to cover the collage evidence with her quilt. "You shouldn't be in my room!" she said.

"I've been telling her that for years," Stephanie said. And with a toss of her golden curls, she left.

"Here's your invitation to my surprise party," Kimmy said, handing D.J. an envelope.

D.J. looked doubtful. "You're throwing yourself a surprise party?"

"Yeah, but don't tell. This is the face I'm gonna use." Kimmy widened her eyes and threw up both hands in mock surprise.

D.J. tore open the envelope and read it aloud. "'You are cordially invited to attend Kimmy's fabulous Fourteenth Birthday Surprise Party at the Excelsior Hotel.'

Whoa." She looked up, impressed. "How'd you swing that?"

Kimmy shrugged and went over to D.J.'s dresser to sample her new Antique Rose blush.

"My brother Garth is a bellhop at the Excelsior," she said. "He can sneak us into the pool area." She turned back to D.J. There were two big, pink Antique Rose circles on Kimmy's cheeks.

D.J. wasn't thrilled. "You're having a pool party in November? What a dweeb idea."

"The hotel has an indoor pool," Kimmy explained. "Tomorrow we can go to the mall and buy new bathing suits. The cruise collections just came out. This party's going to be so rad."

"Rad for *you* maybe," D.J. said. "*You* have the perfect body."

Smugly, Kimmy surveyed her long, thin body. "Well, I can't argue with you there."

"There's no way I'm wearing a bathing suit in public until I'm as skinny as…"—she reached under the quilt and pulled out a magazine cutout—"one of these models." She held up a photograph from the annual swimsuit edition of a popular national sports magazine. The magazine was filled with photographs of the world's skinniest, most beautiful models wearing the world's sheerest, most fashionable swimsuits.

Kimmy's face fell. "But you *have* to come to my party! You're my best friend."

"All right, I'll go," said D.J. hesitantly. "But that means I have only three weeks to get skinny—starting right now." She picked up the bag of cookies and threw it into the wastebasket. Then she looked at Kimmy resentfully. "How do you stay so skinny anyway?"

"Well, I exercise a lot. Like waist-bends, for example." Demonstrating, Kimmy bent over the wastebasket and reached inside. "One, two, three, and four," she counted before straightening up with the bag of cookies in her hand. "And I watch what I eat. See?" Kimmy took a cookie out of the bag and examined it closely. "This looks good."

She ate the cookie whole, crunching it loudly while D.J. groaned.

Fifty-five seconds into her new diet and D.J. already had a whopping case of the Weight-Loser's Blues.

# TWO

**The next afternoon,** D.J. was in the kitchen taping another kind of collage to the refrigerator door. Rebecca came in through the back door.

"Whoa," Rebecca said, pulling up short. "I bet your dad and the guys will like that better than Michelle's finger paintings."

D.J. stared at the collage she had created. It was made up entirely of swimsuit models.

"This will inspire me to stay on my new crash diet," she said.

Rebecca worked with D.J.'s father, Danny, at the local television show, *Wake Up, San Francisco*. Rebecca was also engaged to D.J.'s uncle Jesse.

"You don't need to go on a crash diet," Rebecca said in a motherly tone. "If you want to drop a pound or two, just eat sensibly."

D.J. rolled her eyes. Rebecca didn't understand. If Rebecca had to appear in a bathing suit in three weeks, she'd look terrific. She was almost as skinny as the swimsuit models.

"Believe me," D.J. said. "I need a crash diet."

But Rebecca had already launched into her lecture. "Eating sensibly means you can have fish, chicken without the skin, fruits, and vegetables. Just tell your father not to buy any more junk food."

Just then, Uncle Jesse came in the back door carrying a big box. "Cake's here!" he called out cheerfully.

"All right!" Rebecca said. "Let me at it!" Then, remembering her lecture to D.J., she said, "Jess, maybe we should do this later."

But D.J. didn't need any special treatment. "It's okay, Becky," she said. "I don't need any cake."

Jesse gave her a look. He knew his niece had a sweet tooth as powerful as his own love of the Late Great Elvis. But he wasn't going to bring it up.

Determinedly, D.J. opened the door to the freezer. "I'll just have one of these delicious water pops I made," she said.

Jesse shrugged, and then yelled, "Hey, everybody! Get in the kitchen! I need some opinions!"

Silence.

He tried again. "Free cake!"

Danny, Joey, and Stephanie came stampeding through the swinging door from the living room. Four-year-old Michelle, the youngest Tanner, scrambled at their heels. Then, as always, she squeezed her way to the front of the line. "I'm here!" she announced cheerfully.

How had this group come to live together under one roof? It all began a little over three years ago, not long after the three girls' mother died in a car accident. Uncle Jesse and his best friend, Joey, had moved in to help Danny raise D.J., Stephanie, and Michelle. The girls got used to having the guys around—it was like having three fathers! And Danny certainly had appreciated the help. It was a full house, all right. And soon, after the wedding, Rebecca would be moving in with Jesse. Then the house would change from full to bursting. But no one was complaining. If full meant fun, fuller could only mean "funner," right?

"All right," Jesse said to the group. "I want you all to help Becky and me choose our wedding cake."

"Jess," his fiancée said, "aren't you jumping the gun? We haven't even picked the date."

"Hey," Jesse said, "first we pick the cake,

then we pick the date. Get your priorities in order, woman."

"Didn't we agree on chocolate?" said Rebecca. As far as wedding plans went, this was about all they had agreed on so far.

"We did," Jesse said. "But chocolate's not just chocolate anymore." He opened the big box. Everyone peered inside and saw several dozen small chocolate cake squares. Michelle's mouth dropped. "Whoa baby!" she said. She couldn't wait for a taste or two...or three. Everyone else felt the same.

"The baker gave us samples of the chocolate we have to choose from," Jesse explained. "We've got your dark chocolate, Dutch chocolate, white chocolate, Jamoca choco chocolate, double-fudge chocolate, triple chocolate-chocolate-chocolate and . . ."—he took a deep breath—"carrot cake. I felt sorry for it. It looked so lonely on the shelf. Nobody ever picks carrot cake."

Michelle reached into the box for a sample. One by one, the others did the same. Joey noticed D.J. standing off by herself sucking on a water pop. "Come on, Deej," he said. "You're gonna miss the cake."

"Who needs cake when you can lick ice on a stick?" she said, trying to sound enthused. "Mmmmmm. Wet and cold and . . . that's about it."

"Now the plan is," Jesse was saying, "everybody taste everything and tell me what you like best. Which do you like, Michelle?"

Michelle, whose face was smeared with chocolate from ear to ear, grinned. "I like chocolate the best!"

Stephanie reached for her flute. "This calls for a little cake-eating music," she said. "And I just happened to have my instrument handy." Once again, she started playing her own version of "On Top of Old Smokey."

D.J. made a face. It wasn't bad enough she had to miss out on the cakes. Now she had to listen to the world's worst music too. Life just isn't fair, she thought.

# THREE

**Still in her nightgown,** D.J. took a deep breath and stepped onto her bedroom scale.

"I hate this part," she said to Stephanie who stood watching.

"Day three," said Stephanie, speaking into an imaginary microphone. "The diet continues."

D.J. looked down at the scale, and her eyes

widened in disbelief. After three days of practically starving herself, she'd lost only a measly half pound.

"I know what you need," Stephanie said. "You need to be weighed to music."

For the umpteenth time, Stephanie played her favorite tune.

"Have mercy!" cried Jesse, walking in with his hands clamped over his ears. As a part-time musician, he knew good music when he heard it. But, music this *wasn't*, as far as he was concerned. Practice was *not* making perfect in Stephanie's case.

"This can't be right!" D.J. said. "Three days and I've only lost half a pound? I'm going off this stupid diet!"

"Good," Jesse said. "You shouldn't be on a diet anyway. If you want to shape up a little, start exercising. Why don't you come down to the gym where Michelle works out?"

"Oh, yeah—like I really want Michelle's body," D.J. said sarcastically.

"It's not just a kid's gym," said Jesse.

"People of all ages go there. The whole family can go this afternoon to tone up. Of course, in my case," he said, admiring his profile in the mirror, "I'd just be toning tone."

Later that day, Danny was in the kitchen doing one of his favorite things—the dishes. Unlike most guys, Danny Tanner liked to do housework. He preferred it to playing golf, to going fishing, and to just about everything else.

Danny was holding a glass that he had just rinsed up to the light to admire its shine when Kimmy came in without knocking. She had a shopping bag hanging over one shoulder.

"Another big Saturday with the dishes, Mr. T.?" she said.

Danny smiled tolerantly, wishing she wouldn't call him Mr. T. "Nice to see you, too, Kimmy," he said.

"Hey, Kimmy," said D.J., who was coming downstairs. "I thought I heard you. What's in the bag?"

"Hey, D.J.," her father said before Kimmy could answer her, "you missed lunch, so I saved you a sandwich."

"Great," D.J. said without enthusiasm. "Thanks."

"Check out my new swimsuit," said Kimmy. She held up a neon-orange bikini.

D.J. made no comment, looking more discouraged than ever.

But Danny couldn't resist. "That swimsuit is you, Kimmy. It's loud." Then he looked at D.J. "Sit down and eat up, Deej," he said. "We're going to the gym." He left the room to get ready.

D.J. plunked herself down at the table. She lifted the top piece of bread from the sandwich and then lowered it. "You want my sandwich, Kimmy?"

"Sure." Kimmy took the sandwich and checked it out for herself. "Ham again?"

Just then, Stephanie came down the stairs to get a cookie. With D.J. on a diet, there was a surplus these days.

Kimmy passed the sandwich back to D.J.

"I've been eating your lunch for three days now, and every sandwich is boiled ham. Did your dad hit a pig with his car?" Then she picked up the shopping bag and left for home.

"See you, Kimmy!" D.J. called out with a sigh.

Stephanie chewed her cookie thoughtfully. "D.J., you've been giving your lunches to Kimmy?"

"Yeah, so what?"

Stephanie nodded slowly. "But you've been skipping breakfast and dinner too. I'm not an expert on this, but shouldn't a person eat?"

Great! All D.J. needed was her kid sister monitoring her food intake. "Okay, okay, I'll eat my sandwich," she said.

Stephanie stood and waited. "Promise?"

"Promise." D.J. picked up the sandwich and took a bite.

"Much better," said Stephanie. "Now get yourself an apple and a glass of milk and all your basic food groups will be covered."

Stephanie shook crumbs off her hands and marched toward the stairs.

As soon as Stephanie started up the stairs, D.J. spit out the bite of sandwich she'd taken, into a napkin.

"Look what I got for you, Comet!" she whispered to the family dog. "People food." D.J. dropped the sandwich into the dog's bowl, too engrossed in what she was doing to notice Stephanie watching her from the stairs. "You're lucky," D.J. told Comet. "Dogs don't have to wear bathing suits."

Stephanie marched right back into the kitchen. "D.J.," she said, "you promised you'd eat your sandwich. You lied."

Embarrassed, D.J. thought fast. "Comet stole it right out of my hand," she said.

"You're lying again." Stephanie wasn't going to let her sister get away with this.

"No, I'm not," D.J. said defensively.

"Yes, you are! Lie number three. When will it ever end?" Stephanie flung up her arms dramatically.

"Look, Stef," D.J. said desperately. "I've

18

got two weeks to get skinny. I have to look good in a bathing suit at Kimmy's pool party—in front of all my friends. After the party I'll start eating again. But until then, this is our secret. Now give me your pinky."

"No! Not the pinky!" Stephanie took a step backward.

"Yes, the pinky," D.J. said sternly. "You've got to pinky-swear you won't tell anyone I haven't been eating. Now hook up."

Reluctantly, Stephanie extended her right hand, pinky first.

"Now say it," D.J. demanded. "'Pinky-swear.'"

"Pinky-swear." Stephanie said, frowning. "But I don't like it."

"Too bad," D.J. told her. "Your lips are zipped."

# FOUR

**The Tanner contingent,** in brightly colored workout gear, entered the gym. The place was really jumping. An aerobics class was in full swing, and the exercise machines were almost all being used.

Stephanie stalled in the doorway and wrinkled her nose. "It smells like a sweat sock in here," she said.

"Yeah," Joey said, breathing in deeply. "These are my people."

A real Arnold Schwarzenegger type strolled past, muscles rippling.

"What do you bench, dude?" Joey asked him.

"Five-oh-five," the muscle guy said casually.

"Beginner, huh?" Joey said, nodding. "It's cool."

"Yeah, right," the muscle guy sneered. He twitched a bicep in Joey's face and walked away.

"Hey, mister!" Michelle called after him. "You are very lumpy!"

Jesse grabbed Michelle and covered her tiny mouth with his hand. Then he looked up and gave the guy a weak smile. "I hope you're not offended, sir," he said, "but if you are, that's her father over there." He pointed to Danny.

Danny smiled his best seventy-pound-weakling smile and waved.

The muscle guy waved back. "No hard

feelings," he said, climbing onto the tread-mill.

D.J. stood watching, hands on hips, in baggy sweats and a sweatband. She looked around at the many rows of exercise equipment, gleaming like instruments in a modern torture chamber. Well, nobody ever said it was going to be easy!

"What's the best way to burn calories?" she asked her father.

"Make it fun," Danny suggested. "Ride one of these bikes. I loved bike riding when I was a kid."

D.J. climbed onto a shiny stationary bicycle. Danny began to fiddle with the complicated controls. "Of course," he added with a little laugh. "My banana-seat Huffy didn't have an onboard computer."

D.J. started to pedal.

"Start off slow, on level one, okay?" Rebecca said. "Don't do too much too soon."

D.J. nodded, pedaling away.

"Come on, Stef," Rebecca said. "Let's go stretch before the next aerobics class." And they headed over to an area with lots of mats.

"To the kiddie gym, boys," Michelle said. "Follow me. One, two, one, two." Danny, Jesse, and Joey fell into line and followed. They looked like young army recruits marching behind the world's shortest drill sergeant.

# FIVE

**The kiddie gym** had a mini-trampoline, tumbling mats, a balance beam, and rings—everything a budding gymnast would need to become an Olympic gold-medal winner. Her pigtails bobbing, Michelle dashed in ahead of the guys as if she owned the place.

"Hi Zachary...hi Kelsey...hi kid-I-don't-know," she called to her little friends,

24

all four and five years old. Some of them were gathering together for their weekly tumbling class. They were all dressed in adorable little leotards, tights, and leg-warmers, looking like a Munchkin version of a Jane Fonda workout class.

"Show us your stuff, Michelle," Uncle Jesse said.

"I'm ready, Freddie," Michelle called out.

"Okay," Joey said, pretending to speak into a sportscaster microphone. "Michelle Tanner is about to begin the Iron Munchkin Triathlon. First event: trampoline.

Michelle hopped up on the mini-tramp. "I love this!" she cried, bouncing into the air.

"Let's see that again in slow motion," Joey called.

Michelle bounced very slowly and switched her voice to low speed.

"I l-o-o-o-v-ve th-i-i-i-s," she yelled. Danny and Jesse cheered.

"Next event, the balance beam," Joey said. "The excitement is intense."

Michelle climbed onto the beam, which was only six inches off the floor.

"Remember," Joey reminded Danny, Jesse, and an imaginary audience, "she's working without a net. And for the big finish, Michelle will attempt a single-tuck somersault with no twist. We must have complete silence while she prepares."

Michelle closed her eyes and took a deep breath.

"She's psyching up...and there she goes!"

Michelle's crooked somersault was met with cheerful applause.

"A perfect ten!" said her father, as if he were the judge.

"I am pumped!" Michelle declared, and flexed her little bicep.

Meanwhile, back in the torture chamber, D.J. had switched from the bike to the stair-step machine. She had done exactly what Rebecca told her not to do—turned the dial up to the most difficult level.

Pale and drenched with sweat, she climbed the mechanical steps. Every time her energy lagged, she thought of those skinny, long-legged models in their bathing suits. She would get that skinny. She just *had* to!

Stephanie dashed in. "D.J., you've got to come to aerobics class," she said. "It's so much fun! The instructor plays the coolest rock music."

"I'll be right there," D.J. said, panting.

Stephanie's smile faded. D.J. didn't look too good. In fact, she looked kind of sick. Before Stephanie could say anything, D.J. collapsed like a rag doll down onto the stairs. The machine ground to a halt. Stephanie screamed.

One of the gym attendants came running. He picked up D.J.'s limp hand and felt for her pulse. "Go fill this up with water," he said to Stephanie, handing her a plastic cup. "She'll be okay—she just fainted."

Stephanie rushed over to the water fountain, where she saw Joey. Breathlessly, she told him what had happened, and he rushed back into the kiddie gym to get Danny and Jesse.

By the time the guys arrived, D.J. was sitting up on a bench, sipping the water.

"You're sure you're okay?" Danny asked, sounding extremely worried.

D.J. managed a weak smile. "I'll live," she said. "Honest. Guess I just overdid it."

She stood up but got dizzy again and had to sit back down.

"I think we'd better get Michelle and go home," Danny said quietly.

Everybody nodded. Suddenly, they all looked tired.

# SIX

**"Will you still** do this after we're married?" Rebecca asked sweetly.

Jesse was massaging his fiancée's feet as they sat in the kitchen. Joey was at the stove cooking up one of his special dishes for Saturday night dinner, and Danny and Stephanie were setting the table. D.J. trudged downstairs from her bedroom.

"Hi, guys," she said.

"Are you feeling better after your nap, honey?" Danny asked. He was folding the napkins into neat little steeples.

"Yep, I'm as good as new," D.J. said.

"You sure?" Rebecca asked.

"Yeah, I'm sure."

"Are you sure you're sure?" Stephanie asked for good measure.

That did it! "Would everybody quit making such a big deal!" D.J. exploded.

"Hey Deej," Joey called over to her, "I'm making your favorite. Chicken parmesan. This sauce is my best yet. Want to taste?" He held out a wooden spoon filled with red sauce.

D.J. stared at it longingly. Joey's marinara sauce was primo. "I can't," she said, backing off. "I just brushed my teeth."

"Before dinner?" Danny asked.

"Doesn't anyone care about dental hygiene around here?" D.J. said.

"Whoa, calm down. I, of all people, care

deeply about our family's teeth and gums," her father said.

Just then Michelle skipped in from the living room carrying Stephanie's flute.

"I can play," she boasted. "Listen." And she tooted a totally tuneless tune.

D.J. plugged her ears. "Will you please stop that noise?" she hollered.

Michelle ignored her and played on.

"I can't take it anymore!" D.J. yelled. She reached over and snatched the instrument right out of her little sister's mouth.

"Hey, mister!"—Michelle stamped her foot—"I was playing!"

"D.J.!" Danny said in astonishment. Was this the D.J. he knew and loved? "What's going *on* with you?"

"Nothing's going on." She unfolded a napkin steeple. "I'm going to Kimmy's for dinner."

"Don't believe her, Dad," Stephanie piped up.

D.J. shot her sister a look: traitor!

"Really, Dad," Stephanie boldly continued. "It's not true."

"Stephanie, you promised!" D.J. cried. She held up her pinky as a stern reminder.

"I don't care anymore," said Stephanie. "Dad, I know why D.J.'s acting so cranky and why she got dizzy today. She hasn't eaten anything in days."

Danny turned to D.J. "Is that true?" he asked quietly.

"Of course it's not true," D.J. sputtered. "Yesterday, I had a stalk of celery . . . and cottage cheese."

"Four spoonfuls of cottage cheese," said Stephanie, holding up four fingers.

"Five!" D.J. held up four fingers and her thumb.

But Danny didn't care how many spoonfuls his eldest daughter had eaten. "Is what Stephanie's saying true?" he asked D.J.

D.J. tried to meet her father's big, brown trusting eyes. But it was awfully hard to do anything but tell the truth.

"What, Michelle?" Stephanie asked in an exaggeratedly loud voice. "Do you want me to take you upstairs and teach you how to play 'On Top of Old Smokey'—with feeling?"

"I didn't say that," said a puzzled Michelle.

"But someday you might," said Stephanie, and she grabbed Michelle's hand and dragged her upstairs.

Jesse, Joey, Danny, and Rebecca were all staring at D.J. "You'd better sit down and eat some dinner right now," Jesse said.

D.J. stood her ground. "I can't. I'm finally starting to lose weight."

"D.J., you're starving yourself," said Danny. "You can do real damage to your body."

"Sweetheart," Rebecca added gently, "this kind of behavior can lead to serious eating disorders. You're headed for trouble if you keep this up."

"She's right, Deej," Joey put in.

"I don't care," D.J. said, backing away from them all. "I have to wear a bathing suit next week and I have to put it on a skinny body. This is my life and I can do whatever I want!"

She turned around and ran upstairs in tears.

# SEVEN

**Michelle had gone off** to her own room to "practice" the flute. Stephanie was huddled on her bed with fuzzy Mr. Bear. They were having a philosophical discussion, the subject being: what happens when you break a pinky-swear? Stephanie had a feeling she was about to find out.

D.J. stormed into the room. "How could you tell on me?" she demanded.

35

Stephanie clutched Mr. Bear tighter. Her chin trembled. "I was scared," she said. "I didn't want you to get sick or faint again."

"Why don't you mind your own business!" said D.J. angrily.

"Because she loves you," Danny said from the doorway. "And you're very lucky to have her for a sister."

Stephanie got down from her bed, still holding Mr. Bear. "Please don't be mad at me," she begged her sister in a small pitiful voice. Then she crept out of the room.

"D.J.," Danny began.

But D.J. held up her hand. She didn't want to hear it. "Dad, you don't understand," she said. "I don't like the way I look. I want to look like those models." She pointed to the photographs of models she had tacked to her bulletin board.

Danny walked over and looked at them, taking his time. "Why?" he finally asked.

*Why*? Sometimes her dear, sweet father could be so amazingly dense! "Because they're beautiful—that's why," she told him.

36

Danny turned to her. "So are you," he said simply.

D.J. rolled her eyes. "You're just saying that because you're my father."

"I'm saying it because it's true," he said.

"Oh yeah? Show me one girl up there with this round face." D.J. pinched her own cheeks. "See these? These are chipmunk cheeks. I hate them!"

Danny smiled gently and folded his lanky body into a kid-sized chair. He pulled it up to the kid-sized table and folded his hands neatly on top.

"Honey," he said, "people come in all shapes and sizes. Everyone wishes they could change something about themselves. When I was a kid I wished I could be like the guy from *The Incredible Hulk*."

D.J. nearly laughed out loud. "You wanted to be a big green monster with muscles?" she asked.

"No, the other guy. The guy who turns into the Hulk—Bill Bixby. He was nice and average. He wasn't too skinny. He wasn't too tall. He didn't stick out like I thought I did. But then I realized that that guy didn't have it so easy. Every time he lost his temper he had to buy a new shirt."

D.J. smiled in spite of herself. "Dad, there's no way I'm going to wear a bathing suit in front of all my friends."

"D.J., let me ask you something. Why do you like your friends?"

D.J. thought for a moment. "Because they're nice and we do fun stuff together."

"Not because they all look like models?" said Danny, knowingly.

D.J. was beginning to get the picture. "No," she said.

"Maybe it's because, deep down inside, you know that how a person looks on the outside isn't nearly as important as who they are on the inside," said her father. "Right?"

D.J. hated to admit it, but her dad was right. She hesitated a moment and then nodded in agreement.

"I think you should see yourself in the same way you see your friends," Danny continued. "Sweetheart, you have a good heart. You care about people. That's why people care about you. And everyone who knows the real D.J. thinks she's pretty terrific."

He was pretty terrific himself, D.J. thought, and she went over to give him a hug. "Thanks, Dad," she said. "I love you."

"And I love you," said Danny. "And that's why I want you to take good care of yourself. And promise me you'll eat healthy and exercise the right way."

D.J. nodded and smiled. "I promise. No more crash diets for me. I'll just go to Kimmy's party and have fun with my friends."

"That's great," said Danny. "Anything else you want to talk about?"

D.J.'s stomach growled loud enough for them both to hear. That chicken parmesan sure smelled good!

"Yeah." She grinned. "When do we eat?"

# EIGHT

**Late Monday afternoon,** Rebecca was sitting at the kitchen table flipping through the newspaper. Jesse hovered impatiently over her shoulder.

"Are you sure your wedding announcement is in today's paper?" asked Danny as he poured himself a cup of coffee.

"It better be," Jesse said. "I ordered thirty extra copies to send to all my relatives."

Rebecca flattened the paper on the table. "Here it is! Oh, this is so wonderful!" she said excitedly.

Suddenly, her expression changed and she quickly flipped pages to the sports section. "So how about those 49ers?" she marveled.

Jesse grabbed the paper from her. "Let me see that."

"No, Jesse," said Rebecca, closing her eyes. "Believe me. You don't want to see it."

But Jesse had already found his way back to the society section. He read aloud: "'Rebecca Donaldson, award-winning journalist and popular star of *Wake Up, San Francisco*, to wed Jerzy . . .'—Jerzy!" Jesse was furious.

Danny laughed. "I guess you do look more like a Jerzy than a Jesse. Great mistake on their part."

"Don't worry," Rebecca said breezily. "Nobody ever reads that stuff anyhow."

Joey came upstairs from his basement bedroom. "Hi, Danny," he said. "Hi, Becky." Pause. "Hi, Jerzy."

Jesse growled.

Joey went over to the refrigerator to take out sandwich makings.

Stephanie came in through the back door wearing a black and yellow striped uniform. She had just been at her weekly after-school Honeybee meeting. She flung her Honeybee backpack on the table in disgust.

"That's it! I quit!" she exclaimed. "I'm way too mature for those dodo-head Honeybees."

"Stef," her father said. "You can't quit. I just spent eighteen dollars for that new pollen backpack."

"There's no way I'm going to that dumb Honeybee slumber party on Saturday night!" Stephanie cried, and ran upstairs.

Jesse, his own problems forgotten, stared after his niece, scratching his head. "What was *that* all about?" he said.

Danny nodded thoughtfully. "I think I

know. That slumber party's for mothers and daughters. I remember when Pam took D.J."

Joey carried his sandwich to the table. "Poor Stef," he sympathized.

But Danny's face lit up. He had an idea. "I know this is a lot to ask," he began, looking at Rebecca.

Rebecca understood immediately. "Hey, Danny, it's no problem. I would love to take Stephanie to the slumber party. I'm going to be in Lake Tahoe Saturday, but I'll be back in plenty of time."

"Thanks, Becky," Danny said.

As Rebecca headed upstairs to tell Stephanie the good news, she met Michelle coming down.

"Hi, Becky," Michelle said, waving.

Rebecca waved back. "Hi, Michelle."

At the foot of the stairs, Michelle greeted the three men in her young life: "Hi, Daddy; hi, Joey; hi, Uncle Jerzy."

# NINE

**It was a tight squeeze,** but Stephanie was barely able to close the zipper of her overnight bag without pinching Mr. Bear's fur.

D.J., who stood at the dresser brushing her hair, watched her sister in the mirror. "Why are you packing now?" she asked. "The slumber party's not for six hours."

Stephanie shrugged. "You know the Honeybee motto—always '*bee*' ready."

D.J. turned to her, and made bug eyes. "Stef, you are so *bee*-zarre."

Just then Kimmy came in rolling a gigantic suitcase, which she parked next to Stephanie's bed. "*Bonjour*, ladies."

"Hi, Kimmy," D.J. said, pulling her hair into a ponytail.

Kimmy jumped onto Stephanie's bed, testing the mattress for firmness. "A little soft," she concluded, "but I can rough it."

"Get your bony bod off my bed," Stephanie griped.

Ignoring her, Kimmy started to unpack: shirts, pants, pajamas, magazines, video-cassettes, diary. This wasn't a sleepover—it was a major installation.

"Oh," D.J. casually told her sister, "did I forget to mention that since you're not gonna be here, Kimmy's sleeping in your bed?"

Stephanie grimaced. "Eeeeeeow. Kimmy in my sheets. Gibbler cooties. I'll get the bug spray." She exited purposefully.

Kimmy continued to unpack. She set her vast array of toiletries on the night table. "Whoa!" she said, picking up the framed picture of Danny. "This could be a pretty scary thing to wake up to."

She laid the picture facedown and replaced it with a framed photo of her own. "Patrick Swayze. Now *that* says 'Good morning'!"

Six hours later, Stephanie knelt on a chair looking out her bedroom window, scanning the darkening street below. Becky should have been here by now. Where was she? Had she forgotten?

"Take it easy," D.J. told her. "She's only ten minutes late. Cheer up. We're just about to go downstairs and begin the Patrick Swayze film festival."

"Yeah," Kimmy put in, "it's 'Crazy for Swayze Night' in Tannertown."

Just then, the phone rang. Comet yipped.

"That's probably Patrick himself," Kimmy said. "Tell him to run—not walk— right over."

46

Stephanie grabbed the phone. "Hello?" she said.

"Stephanie? It's Becky." She sounded far away.

"Becky, where are you?" asked Stephanie nervously. Once D.J. saw that the call wasn't for her, she and Kimmy left the room.

Stephanie heard static on the other end of the line. "I'm stuck in Placerville," Becky said. "My car broke down. I dropped my transmission."

Stephanie tapped her foot impatiently. "Well, pick it up and get over here," she demanded. "We're late for the slumber party."

"Oh, honey," Becky apologized, "I'm so sorry. But the mechanic says my car won't be fixed for another eight hours. It needs a new part which they'll have to get from another garage."

Just Stephanie's luck. "That's okay," she said quietly. "Thanks anyway. Bye." She hung up slowly, feeling tears prickling at the back of her eyes. She wouldn't cry. She wouldn't. She went over to her bed and sat

47

down. Comet followed and rested his muzzle against her knee.

"I didn't want to go to that party, anyway," Stephanie said out loud. "It's just a bunch of girls with their moms. How boring. We'll have much more fun by ourselves. Right, Comet?"

The dog made a sad little whining noise as Stephanie wiped a tear off her cheek. Who wanted to sleep on the floor anyway? Slumber parties were strictly for dodoes.

# TEN

**Stephanie was unpacking** when Joey came in.

"I heard about Rebecca getting stuck in Placerville," he said. "That's too bad, Stef."

"It's okay. I didn't want to go to that slumber party anyway," she said miserably.

"Not even if I take you?" he asked.

49

Stephanie paused with her pajamas in one hand. Had she heard him right? Was he offering to take her to the mother-daughter slumber party?

She turned around and faced him. "*You* take *me*?"

"Hey," Joey said, "I slumber, I party. Why not?"

"Because it's for mothers and daughters—that's why not. You're a boy."

"I won't tell if you won't."

Her jaw dropped. Joey was serious! Could she really show up at the slumber party with Joey?

"C'mon Stef. Your friends all know me." He began to repack the suitcase for her. "They won't mind. Whose house is it at?"

"Lisa's," said Stephanie, watching Joey fold her pajamas.

"Good old Lisa," said Joey. "Now, are we going to the slumber party to have a ton of fun or are we going to stay home and watch Patrick Swayze?" He zipped up her repacked bag and stood back, waiting.

Stephanie frowned. She had her doubts, but Joey seemed so up for it. She didn't want to disappoint him. "Are you sure?"

"Honeybee's honor," Joey said solemnly. Then, to Stephanie's horror, he burst into the Honeybee anthem.

"Okay, okay," she said louder than his singing. "I'll go! But only if you promise not to sing at the party."

Joey stopped and shrugged amiably. "Just getting it out of my system," he said.

A half hour later, Stephanie and Joey stood on Lisa's doorstep.

Lisa opened the door. "Hi, Stef," she said.

"Hi, Lisa," Stephanie replied, peering over her friend's shoulder. She saw little groups of mothers and daughters sitting around the living room—playing with dolls. Dolls! How could she ever have thought that bringing Joey would work?

Obviously, Lisa agreed. "What'd you

bring Joey for?" she asked.

Joey walked in. "Don't mind me," he said. "Tonight, I'm just one of the girls. Hi, ladies!"

"Hi, Joey," said Lisa's mom, Chris, coming over to the door. Chris was the hostess of the party. "Where's Rebecca?"

"She couldn't make it," said Joey. "So I'm the D.H.—Designated Honeybee."

Chris unsuccessfully tried to hide her amusement. "Well, you're just in time for some Barbie."

"Great, throw another shrimp on for me," Joey said, misunderstanding completely.

But Stephanie set him straight. "Joey, that's Barbie *doll*—not barbe-*cue*," she said.

Joey went over to a group of moms and girls dressing their Barbie dolls. "Hey, it's Malibu Barbie! Whoa!" He did his Valley Girl imitation. "Like this party's totally gnarly, dude."

Melissa, a freckle-faced Honeybee, scowled up at him. Smoothing her doll's hair, she said. "That's *not* Malibu Barbie. That's *Superstar* Barbie."

Stephanie slapped her forehead.

"My mistake," Joey apologized. "I'm really more of a Ken kinda guy myself."

He picked up the nearest Ken doll and walked him over to meet Superstar Barbie.

"So Superstar, we've got a lot in common. We've both got plastic heads, we can't blink, and we have no internal organs."

Stephanie yanked Joey's arm and whispered, "Joey, cut it out."

Joey smiled nervously. All eyes were on him. Nobody was laughing at his little skit. Barbies were serious business, and here he was making fun of them.

It was going to be the longest slumber party in history.

# ELEVEN

**By the time** the egg-and-spoon contest rolled around, Joey was in his jumbo-sized Teenage Mutant Ninja Turtles pajamas. They had already played jacks and jumped rope. Would the fun never end?

Chris clapped her hands together. "Okay, girls, mothers . . ."—she floundered when she saw Joey, then continued—"big people, uh, line up here."

All mothers, daughters, and Joey did just that.

"The object of this game," Chris explained, "is to race around the room with an egg in a spoon, without dropping the egg."

"Piece of cake," Joey whispered to Stephanie. After the double-dutch jump-rope session, how hard could it be to carry an egg around?

"But the tough part," Chris went on, "is, we'll be wearing high heels."

Stephanie's jaw dropped. Joey merely chuckled. "Silly old me," he said. "I left my high heels at home."

Chris thrust a pair of red spiked heels at Joey. They weren't exactly a men's size 12, but they would have to do.

Joey managed a weak smile, looking a little sick. "Oh good," he said, holding up the shoes. "And they complement my outfit too."

Chris handed high heels to mothers and

daughters. "Okay," she continued. "Girls first. Once around the coffee table, back to the starting line, then pass off the eggs and the spoons to your mothers—or Joey."

The girls stood in their high heels, each clutching an egg-bearing spoon.

"Ready, set, go!" Chris shouted.

The girls set out, wobbling like crazy. Only Stephanie seemed to handle the high heels with any skill. She took the lead and kept it.

"Go, Stef, go!" Joey yelled above the din of screaming, cheering moms.

Stephanie crossed the line and handed the egg off to Joey. They were ahead by several feet.

"Go, Joey, go!" Stephanie shouted. Now it was her turn to be the cheering section.

But Joey was nothing to cheer at, stumbling across the floor in his too small, too high heels.

The mothers, used to wearing high heels, left Joey in the dust; and long after the slowest mother, he wibble-wobbled over the finish line.

"Aw, Joey!" Stephanie's disappointment was obvious.

"Sorry, Stef," Joey apologized.

Stephanie shook her head regretfully. The evening just kept getting worse and worse.

Just then, Lisa clapped her hands. "Okay, let's play beauty parlor! Daughters make up moms, then moms make up daughters."

"Great idea!" the mothers cheered.

"Yeah!" the daughters joined in.

Stephanie looked doubtfully at Joey. Joey tried to muster up some enthusiasm.

"You know, I've been looking for a way to bring out my cheekbones," he said.

Chris got the message. "Oh, why don't we skip beauty parlor and play something else? Like charades!"

Everybody groaned. Some even booed. Everybody was up for beauty parlor, but no one wanted to play charades.

"I want to do make-overs!" Lisa whined.

Suddenly, Stephanie felt all eyes on her. The slumber party was turning out to be no fun at all. And it was her fault. She should never have let Joey talk her into coming with him. She had no business being here without a mother.

"We can't do make-overs," she said in a tight voice, "because of *me*."

Before anyone could stop her, she ran out the door in her pajamas. Good thing she lived only two doors away.

# TWELVE

**Danny and Jesse** had just come downstairs from tucking in Michelle when
Stephanie burst through the front door. Joey
wasn't far behind.

"Stephanie!" Danny called out.

"Stef!" Joey said. "Would you please stop
and talk to me?"

Stephanie turned. "There's nothing to talk

about. I don't have a mother, and there's nothing you guys can say to change that."

Joey, Danny, and Jesse stared at each other speechlessly. She had them there.

Stephanie nodded her head. "See? I knew it."

She turned and ran through the kitchen and up the stairs.

D.J. and Kimmy were pigging out on junk food on Stephanie's bed. D.J.'s diet was definitely a thing of the past.

"I want my bed back," Stephanie demanded breathlessly.

D.J. paused, about to pop a Cheesy Yum Yum into her mouth. "You're supposed to be gone tonight."

"It was a stupid party, with stupid people and stupid mother-daughter make-overs," Stephanie said.

D.J. nodded, understanding. She signaled to Kimmy, and Kimmy rose with a sigh.

"I can take a hint. Give me a call at home," she said to D.J. "I'll get my stuff tomorrow."

She quietly slipped out the door.

"I'm sorry you had such a bad time," D.J. said carefully. "I know exactly how you feel."

"No, you don't," Stephanie shot back. She picked up her pillow and shook out potato-chip crumbs. "When you were eight, you got to go to the Honeybee slumber party with Mom."

"That doesn't mean I don't miss her just as much as you do," D.J. pointed out gently. She got up and helped Stephanie shake crumbs out of the bedspread.

"It's not fair," Stephanie said. "All those girls with their moms were so happy. Why couldn't I be happy too?" Her voice cracked. She coughed to hide it.

D.J. came around the bed and put her arm around her sister. "It's okay. Sometimes I look at other girls with their moms and I feel the same way."

Stephanie wiped a tear on her sleeve. "How do you make the feelings go away?" she asked.

"It's hard, but you know what helps me? I think about the special things we have that nobody else has."

"Like what?" Stephanie asked.

"Well, we have three people who really love us. We're the only ones with a dad, an Uncle Jesse, and a Joey. And we have something else."

Stephanie knew what her sister was going to say but she asked anyway. "What?"

D.J. grinned at her fondly. "We have each other." And the two of them hugged each other.

Joey was downstairs on the living room couch feeling sorry for himself. The guys were trying to cheer him up.

"Stephanie must hate me for dragging her to that party," he said.

"Hey"—Danny patted him on the back—"your heart was in the right place."

"Yeah," Jesse agreed. "She's gonna thank you for it—someday."

Just then D.J. and Stephanie came downstairs. D.J. was carrying her overnight bag.

Stephanie went over to Joey. It wasn't his fault he was a boy. "Joey, thanks for taking me to that party tonight."

He blinked up at her. "Boy, 'someday' sure came fast."

"Are you okay, Stef?" her dad asked.

Stephanie smiled for the first time all night. "Yeah. I feel better." To Joey, she said, "I'm sorry I ran out like that. You were playing Barbies, jumping rope, wearing high heels . . . and you did it all for me. Thanks."

"Hey, we Honeybees gotta stick together," Joey said.

Stephanie hugged him.

"Let's go, Stef," D.J. said. "We're going back to the slumber party."

"You sure you want to?" Jesse asked.

"Yeah," Stephanie said, "we're gonna do make-overs together. I get to use her new Antique Rose blush."

"You'll look terrific in it," D.J. told her.

As the sisters headed out the door, Joey called, "Don't forget to bring back my overnight bag in the morning." Then he turned to Danny and Jesse and said, "Those are two pretty amazing kids."

The other guys nodded. There was definitely no arguing with that.

# THIRTEEN

**The Monday after** the Honeybee slumber party, Stephanie was eating a snack in the kitchen. Danny and Michelle came in from the afternoon preschool session.

Michelle marched up to Stephanie. "Want to see what I got?" she asked.

Stephanie shrugged. "Sure, why not?"

"You have to say 'please'," said Michelle.

Stephanie looked bored. "I'm not *that* interested."

"Then say, 'No, thank you, Michelle,'" Michelle directed.

Stephanie raised an eyebrow at the little squirt.

"Play along, Stef," Danny said. "It's Politeness Week at Michelle's school. Meet Officer Michelle of the Polite Police."

Michelle whipped off her coat. Taped to her dress was a large silver-colored paper badge.

Stephanie gave Michelle a limp salute.

Michelle jabbed a finger at her: "I'll be watching you, mister!"

Just then D.J. and Kimmy came in. D.J. put her books down on the table, rushed over to Danny, and planted a kiss on his cheek. Danny looked somewhat surprised. "Boy, I missed you, Dad!" she said.

Kimmy helped herself to an after-school snack of ice cream and potato chips.

"And how's the greatest-dad-in-the-history-of-dads feeling today?" D.J. wanted to know.

Danny cocked his head. "Suspicious," he said.

D.J. pulled a chair out from the kitchen table. "Have a seat, Dad. Make yourself comfortable."

"Careful, Dad," Stephanie warned. "She wants money—and lots of it."

D.J. stared at her sister. "How did you know?" she asked.

"Deej, we go back eight years," said Stephanie. "Face it—we all know when it's kiss-up time."

Stephanie finished her snack and left D.J. to her begging.

"All right . . ."—Danny took out his wallet—"how much?"

"Dad, this money's not for anything fun. It's for clothing—a basic necessity of life."

Danny opened his wallet and repeated, "How much?"

"Before I tell you the actual dollar amount, you should know that it's going toward the world's coolest tennis shoes."

"How much?" Danny was growing impatient.

"Only eighty dollars—per shoe."

Danny doubled over, laughing.

Uneasily, D.J. joined in, and so did Kimmy. Suddenly D.J. froze. "Why are we laughing?" she asked insecurely.

"Because . . ."—Danny got a grip on himself—"for a second there, I actually thought you asked for a hundred and sixty dollars for sneakers."

"I did," said D.J.

Danny put his wallet away.

Now it was Kimmy's turn. "But these aren't just sneakers, Mr. T.—these are Blow-Outs."

"Blow-Outs are so rad," D.J. added, her voice rising with excitement. "They actually inhale and exhale as you walk. If I don't get them," she added desperately, "I'm going to be a total geek."

"You know how *that* feels, Mr. T.," Kimmy added, being her usual tactful self.

"It takes one to know one," Danny shot back sweetly. Then he turned back to D.J., who braced herself for a lecture.

"Honey," he began, "you don't always have to follow the crowd. When I was a boy and everyone was wasting their allowance on Evel Knievel jumpsuits, I went out and bought some sensible Sansabelt pants with an adjustable waistband. It's a style still worn by some of America's finest bowlers."

D.J. sighed and exchanged a look with Kimmy. "Time for Plan B," she said. "Dad, wouldn't it be great if I never had to weasel money out of you again?"

"I like Plan B so far," Danny said, smiling.

"What if I earned my own money by getting a job?" said D.J. hopefully. "There's a photographer at the mall who said I could be a part-time assistant."

Danny looked doubtful. Working at the mall? It sounded like serious business. More serious than the occasional babysitting job—that was for sure.

"What about your schoolwork?" he said. "Hasn't your science grade been slipping lately?"

"Mr. T.," Kimmy put in, "I give you my

own personal guarantee that D.J. will raise her grade in science."

Danny stared at Kimmy blankly. "Oh, well, the Gibbler Guarantee—that changes everything."

"Come on, Dad," D.J. said, pressing her palms together. Any minute, she would drop to her knees and just plain beg. "I'm fourteen years old. I'm ready for adult responsibility."

Danny spent a long moment looking at his eldest daughter. She was all eagerness. How could he say no? "Well, all right," he finally agreed.

D.J. jumped up and down clapping.

"As long as you keep on top of your schoolwork," he added, "you can take the job."

What a dad! D.J. hugged him. Even Kimmy came across with a small hug.

"What are you so happy about?" Danny asked Kimmy.

She gave him a wide grin. "D.J.'s getting Blow-Outs. And we have the same size feet! Yes!"

# FOURTEEN

**It was D.J.'s** first day on the job. She sat behind a screen listening to a nervous mother trying to get her young son to smile.

"Come on, Anthony. Please smile for Mommy," she begged. "Pretty please with Ninja Turtles on top?"

Little Anthony scowled and folded his arms across his chest.

71

Jack, the photographer, looked into his camera lens and sighed. Then he raised a hand toward D.J. "Oh, Happy Helper!" he called.

D.J. came out from behind the screen. She wore red-striped tights, a dress with a pinafore, and a curly red wig, and her face was painted. She was supposed to look like Raggedy Ann, but she felt more like Bozo the Clown.

"Excuse me, sir," she said, "but do I really have to wear this every day?"

"That's your official Tot Shot uniform, Tanner. Wear it with pride."

Yeah right, thought D.J. "Then why aren't you wearing one, sir?" she asked politely.

"I'm the boss," he said. "Why should *I* look like a jerk? Now go get Anthony to give us a big Tot Shot smile."

D.J. approached the glum little boy and smiled. "Hi, Anthony, I'm D.J., the Happy Helper. How about a big smile for the camera?"

"No!" he said stubbornly.

D.J. made a variety of funny faces. No luck.

"I know what you need," D.J. said. She went to a trunk of photographer's props and came back with a goofy-looking stuffed animal. In a Munchkin voice, she said, "Hi, I'm Howie Hippo, see me go zippo, I can do a flippo . . . I—" She broke off, seeing it was useless. "Look, kid," she said in a tired voice, "I've had a rough week. Why don't you tell me what I can do to make you laugh?"

She hoped the kid wouldn't ask her for the impossible—like standing on her head and whistling. Or illegal—like robbing a bank.

"Be a duck," said Anthony.

"Oh c'mon," whined D.J., "I'm already a clown."

The photographer tapped his toe impatiently. Other mothers were waiting on line to have their kids photographed.

Reluctantly, D.J. got down and waddled like a duck. She even quacked. "Quack, quack, quack."

Anthony pointed at her and started to laugh. Jack snapped the picture.

"Oh, what a beautiful child," Jack gushed. "Will that be cash or charge?" He went off to ring up the sale. D.J. rose and dusted off her striped knees.

"Oh Happy Helper!" a familiar voice called.

D.J. turned to see Kimmy. When Kimmy took in the full effect of the outfit and the face paint, she burst out laughing.

"Kimmy, do you have to laugh *that* hard?"

Kimmy caught herself. "I'm not laughing at you. I'm laughing *because* of you. No, seriously, isn't it time for a break? There are some cute guys down the way who want to buy us pizza."

D.J. edged toward the screen nervously. "I don't want anybody cute to see me like this," she said.

"Then what about after work?" asked Kimmy.

Wearily, D.J. picked up a stray stuffed elephant. "After work I've got to go straight home, eat dinner, and try to stay awake long enough to study for my science test."

"Poor kid," Kimmy said soothingly. "You're working like a dog and dressing like a dweeb. You must want those Blow-Outs awfully bad."

# FIFTEEN

**"Comet,** it's not polite to beg," said Michelle. "Now say 'please'!"

Michelle held a dog biscuit over Comet's head. Comet barked. "Very good, Comet."

D.J. and Kimmy came in from school. D.J. had a few minutes before she had to get ready to go to work.

"Good afternoon, ladies," Michelle bid them politely.

The big girls returned her greeting.

"Is Dad home yet?" D.J. asked.

"No, but thank you for asking," Michelle said.

"Well, at least I'll stay out of trouble for a few more minutes," D.J. grumbled.

"D.J., you don't have to show your dad the science test," Kimmy said.

"Yes, I do. I promised him I'd bring up my grade," D.J. said. "He knows I'm getting my test back today, and when he sees this"—she held up the paper and shook her head—"I'm dead. The first F of my academic life!" She sank into a chair and leaned her elbows on the kitchen table.

Michelle tapped her briskly on the arm. "Excuse me," she said sternly. "No elbows on the table."

D.J. removed her elbows.

"You know," Kimmy said, looking down thoughtfully at the test paper, "now that I look at it, I don't think you got an F."

D.J. laughed shortly. What was Kimmy talking about? Of course she got an F. There it was. In bold red ink at the top of the page.

Kimmy leaned down over D.J.'s shoulder, holding a red marker she had gotten from the phone message pad. "I believe you got an . . . A," she said. Before D.J. could stop her, Kimmy made a mark.

D.J. stared at the paper in disbelief. With a single deft stroke, Kimmy had just transformed the F into an A.

"Kimmy, how could you do that?" D.J. groaned.

Kimmy shrugged. "It was nothing, really," she said, smiling.

D.J. glanced at the clock. "I have to go to work." She went to get her ridiculous uniform. "Kimmy, I can't believe you gave me that phony A. You've really messed me up for good. Now I can't show it to my dad."

"Why not?" Kimmy wanted to know. "It's a perfect forgery."

D.J. closed her eyes and counted to ten before she spoke. She was closer than ever to really giving it to Kimmy. "Don't you understand?" she said. "What you did is wrong. It's dishonest—it's deceitful. It . . ." —the paper caught her eye—"really does look like an A, doesn't it?" She slid the test into her backpack and began to get ready for work.

# SIXTEEN

**D.J. was waddling** like a duck, doing double duty for a pair of poker-faced twins. Just as D.J.'s knees were about to give out, the kids finally cracked smiles. D.J. had been on the job only three days, but it felt like three years.

She straightened up slowly and blew a strand of hair out of her eyes. This duck routine was getting old very fast. But the kids loved it. So did her boss.

"Great bit, Tanner," Jack said. And he went off to ring up another sale.

D.J. looked out into the mall and caught sight of her father, Stephanie, and Michelle coming toward the booth.

"Great!" she muttered to herself. "More humiliation!"

Michelle pointed at her. "You look like a bozo!" she said, giggling.

"Is that a mop on your head?" Stephanie asked.

"We were in the neighborhood," Danny said, "so I thought we'd stop by and say hi."

"Hi," D.J. said quickly, wanting them to go. "Thanks for stopping by, but I should get back to work."

"Before you go," said Danny, "wasn't your science test due back today?

D.J. nodded slowly.

"How did you do?" her father asked.

Beneath the clown paint, D.J. felt her face

grow hot. "Fine," she said shortly. "I really should—"

"Come on, Deej," her father coaxed. "Do you have your test paper with you?"

D.J. sighed. With her heart doing little flip-flops, she went to get the test out of her backpack. "But there's something I have to tell you first."

Before she could explain about what Kimmy had done, Danny took the test paper from her. When he looked down, his whole face lit up with pride and joy. D.J.'s heart sank.

"You got an A!" he exclaimed. "Way to go, D.J.! This is going right up on the refrigerator." He folded the test paper neatly and put it into his pocket. "You know, I'm embarrassed to say this," he said, "but I had my doubts. But you showed me that you could hold down a job and actually improve on your schoolwork. I've never been more proud of you." He squeezed her shoulders. "Now what did you have to tell me?"

How could she tell him now? How could

she change all that happiness, pride, and joy into nothing but disappointment?

"Uhm," she began. "Uh . . . there's . . . I wanted to tell you that there's a sale on sponges down at the Broom Barn!"

# SEVENTEEN

**The delicious aroma** of devil's food cake filled the Tanner house. Joey had just taken a fresh batch of cupcakes out of the oven, and Stephanie was tasting the icing.

Rebecca and Jesse sat at the kitchen table debating about where to have their wedding. Jesse was all for staging it at Elvis's mansion in Tennessee. Rebecca had visions of Jesse in a sequined tuxedo and herself in a Marge Simpson beehive hairdo that stood a foot high.

"Can't we have it at my folks' home in Nebraska?" she asked meekly.

Nebraska! Jesse could just see himself getting hitched in some barn. He'd be wearing hee-haw overalls and a straw hat. There'd probably be square dancing at the reception!

"No way!" he said. "Not Nebraska!"

"Why don't you just get married here—in good old San Francisco?" Stephanie suggested sensibly.

The lovebirds stared at each other. San Francisco! Why hadn't they thought of that themselves?

Michelle came in from the living room and watched Stephanie as she spread vanilla icing on the cupcakes with a teaspoon.

"May I lick your icing spoon, *please*?" Michelle asked.

"No, you may not," Stephanie told her.

"But I was polite," Michelle said proudly. "I said 'please.'"

"I was polite, too," said Stephanie. "I said, 'No, you may not.'"

"Guess what?" Michelle tore off her politeness badge. "Politeness week is over." She grabbed Stephanie's spoon and ran out of the room.

Stephanie frowned down into her empty hand. "How rude!" she declared.

Jesse paused at the refrigerator door, noticing D.J.'s test paper for the first time. "Whoa!"

D.J. happened to come downstairs just at that moment. Her bag was packed for Kimmy's pool party. When she saw her uncle looking at her science test, she suddenly didn't feel in the mood to party. She headed toward the door.

"Whoa!" Jesse said again, this time to D.J. It was no use trying to escape.

"Hi, Uncle Jess," she said, trying to look innocent. But she knew it was a lost cause.

"I see you got an A on this paper here," Jesse said.

"Oh," she said. "It was nothing."

Jesse nodded. "I'll bet. Let's hear what an A paper sounds like."

Let's not and say we did, she thought.

" 'Number one,' " Jesse read aloud. " 'Photosynthesis. Photosynthesis is the process by which photos are synthesized. It's very complicated so I won't bore you with details.' Boy," he said to D.J., "I'd like to see what an F paper looked like." He peeled the paper off the refrigerator and took it over to D.J.

D.J. watched him cover part of the A with his fingers, making it into an F again. "Maybe something like that?"

"How did you know?" D.J. said, biting her lip.

"How did I know? Are you kidding?" he said. "I used to change 40s to 90s, zeros to 100s. One time, I actually got away with changing *awful* to *awesome*," he recalled fondly. Then, he grew serious again. "But the point is that what I did was wrong, wrong, wrong. And what you did was wrong, wrong, wrong."

"I know, but Kimmy was the one who changed it!" D.J. knew it was no use arguing. Jesse wasn't letting her off that easily.

"You were the one who didn't say anything," he said. "You know what you have to do with this paper?"

"Keep my mouth shut and don't say anything?" D.J. tried hopefully.

Jesse gave her a look that said: Wrong answer.

"All right." D.J. squared her shoulders. "Where's Dad?"

"In the living room, rotating the couch cushions," he said.

"Remember, D.J.," Danny said when he saw his daughter enter the living room. "Always rotate every twenty-five thousand sits."

"Dad, we need to talk," D.J. said.

Danny stopped fussing with the cushions.

88

Something about her tone told him it wasn't just chitchat.

"Didn't Kimmy want you to be early for her party?" he asked.

She shrugged. "It's okay. This is more important."

More important than Gibbler's Gala? "Okay, honey," he said. "Shoot."

"You know what I like best about you?" she ventured heartily.

"My rugged good looks?" he suggested. He took a seat on a newly rotated cushion and invited her to do the same.

"No, your forgiving nature," she said.

"What did you do?" he asked.

"Here goes," D.J. said. "My science grade was an F. Kimmy changed it to an A."

For a moment, Danny was quiet. Then he said, "I'm guessing she doesn't have authority to do that."

"I'm sorry, Dad," said D.J. sadly. "With work and all my other classes, I didn't have time to study."

"Then you should have come and told me

you were having trouble. We had an under-standing. You wanted to be a responsible adult, and this is the least responsible thing you could have done."

D.J. grabbed a throw pillow for security. "I know," she said miserably. "I just wanted to prove I could earn my own money and buy whatever I wanted."

"Well, that's out the window now because you're gonna quit your job. And there'll be no hanging out at the mall until you pull that grade back up."

D.J. sighed. Actually, it was a relief—now that the truth was out. She definitely wouldn't miss the stupid uniform or wad-dling like a duck. "I'll just go back to being a kid again," she said.

"Deej, there's nothing wrong with being a kid. You've got your whole life to be an adult." Danny put an arm around her, and she snuggled up against him.

"I guess if being an adult means wearing a red mop on your head, then I can handle being a kid a little longer," D.J. said.

"Too bad," Stephanie said, backing through the swinging door from the kitchen. She was carrying a tray of iced cupcakes. "Does that mean I don't get to borrow that outfit for next Halloween?"

"Afraid so, Stef," D.J. said. "I'm quitting my job."

"And in case I forgot to mention it," Danny said to his eldest daughter, "you happen to be a great kid."

"What about me?" Stephanie asked indignantly.

"Me, too! I'm great, too." It was Michelle, carrying a stack of paper cups and a fistful of napkins from the kitchen.

"You're all great kids," said Danny. Jesse came in with a pitcher of milk, and Joey and Rebecca trailed in behind him. Cupcake time!

D.J. took her paycheck out of her pocket. "Guess this is my first and last paycheck," she said.

"Are you going to use it to help pay for those Blow-Outs?" Danny asked.

"Are you kidding?" said D.J. "Pay a hundred and sixty bucks for a pair of shoes! No way! I'm treating everybody to the movies on Sunday."

Everybody liked the sound of that.

"Now you're talking, mister," Michelle said. She was glad Politeness Week was over. Now she could grab the biggest cupcake for herself. Being the littlest in a full house meant you had to be fast.

Suddenly, D.J. remembered the party and jumped up.

"Kimmy will be wondering where I am," she said. Grabbing an extra cupcake for the birthday girl, she dashed toward the door. "See ya, everybody!" She waved good-bye.

"Have fun at the party," her father said.

D.J. grinned. "You know, I think I will!"